Fairy Tale Science

Making a Bridge for the Gingerbread Man

by Sue Gagliardi

www.focusreaders.com

Copyright © 2020 by Focus Readers®, Lake Elmo, MN 55042. All rights reserved. No part of this book may be reproduced or utilized in any form or by any means without written permission from the publisher.

Focus Readers is distributed by North Star Editions:
sales@northstareditions.com | 888-417-0195

Produced for Focus Readers by Red Line Editorial.

Photographs ©: Verock/Shutterstock Images, cover (left), 1 (left); Red Line Editorial, cover (right), 1 (right), 11, 13, 15, 27; bonchan/Shutterstock Images, 4–5, 29; 12qwerty/iStockphoto, 7; gorillaimages/Shutterstock Images, 8; ntzolov/iStockphoto, 16–17; dsharpie/iStockphoto, 18; Sirawit Sittiyuno/Shutterstock Images, 21; Alex Potemkin/iStockphoto, 22; Mik Lav/Shutterstock Images, 25

Library of Congress Cataloging-in-Publication Data
Names: Gagliardi, Sue, 1969- author.
Title: Making a bridge for the Gingerbread Man / by Sue Gagliardi.
Description: Lake Elmo, MN : Focus Readers, 2020. | Series: Fairy tale
   science | Includes index. | Audience: Grades 4–6.
Identifiers: LCCN 2019036053 (print) | LCCN 2019036054 (ebook) | ISBN
   9781644930281 (hardcover) | ISBN 9781644931073 (paperback) | ISBN
   9781644932650 (pdf) | ISBN 9781644931868 (ebook)
Subjects: LCSH: Bridges--Design and construction--Juvenile literature.
Classification: LCC TG148 .G34 2020 (print) | LCC TG148 (ebook) | DDC
   624.2--dc23
LC record available at https://lccn.loc.gov/2019036053
LC ebook record available at https://lccn.loc.gov/2019036054

Printed in the United States of America
Mankato, MN
012020

About the Author

Sue Gagliardi writes fiction, nonfiction, and poetry for children. Her books include *Fairies*, *Get Outside in Winter*, and *Get Outside in Spring*. Her work appears in children's magazines including *Highlights Hello*, *Highlights High Five*, *Ladybug*, and *Spider*. She teaches kindergarten and lives in Pennsylvania with her husband and son.

Table of Contents

CHAPTER 1
The Gingerbread Man 5

CHAPTER 2
Build a Model Bridge 9

Drawbridges 16

CHAPTER 3
Results 19

CHAPTER 4
The Science of Bridges 23

Focus on Making a Bridge • 28
Glossary • 30
To Learn More • 31
Index • 32

Chapter 1

The Gingerbread Man

One day, a woman baked a gingerbread man to eat. She opened the oven door. The gingerbread man jumped out of the oven. He ran out of the house. He did not want to be eaten.

The gingerbread man escaped as the woman opened the oven.

The woman and her husband ran after the gingerbread man. But he was too fast. They could not catch him. A cow and a pig ran after him. A horse and a goat ran after him, too. They all wanted to eat him. But no one could catch the quick gingerbread man.

The gingerbread man came to a river. He had no way to cross it. A sly fox offered to let the gingerbread man ride on his back. Then the fox convinced the

 Red foxes are good swimmers. They mainly eat small rodents and rabbits.

gingerbread man to sit on his nose. The fox opened his mouth. He ate the gingerbread man.

Chapter 2

Build a Model Bridge

If the gingerbread man had used a bridge, the fox would not have eaten him. You will design three model bridges for the gingerbread man. You'll test different materials to build the strongest bridge.

 Many bridges stretch across water to make travel easier.

Each bridge should be at least 12 inches (30 cm) long. The bridges must be able to stand on their own. They should support the weight of at least three rocks without breaking. They should **withstand** the weight for at least one minute.

Materials

- Cardboard
- Cardboard tubes
- Craft sticks
- Aluminum foil
- Tape

- Ruler or measuring tape
- Several heavy books
- Several small rocks
- Timer or stopwatch

Instructions

Making the Bridges

1. Build the first model bridge with cardboard and cardboard tubes. Attach the cardboard together with tape.

2. Build the second model bridge with craft sticks. Attach the sticks together with tape.

Fun Fact

Some bridges have two levels. Cars can cross on both the upper and lower levels.

3. Build the third model bridge with foil. Fold the foil to form a bridge shape. Use books to support each end of the bridge.
4. Measure each bridge. The **span** of each bridge should be at least 12 inches (30 cm) long.

13

Testing the Bridges

1. Place the first bridge on a flat surface.
2. Place a rock in the middle of the bridge. Start the stopwatch.
3. Add two more rocks, one at a time. See if the bridge stays standing.

Fun Fact

The first bridges were made of fallen trees. Today, builders use concrete and steel to construct bridges.

4. If the bridge is still standing after one minute, add more rocks. See how many rocks you can add before the bridge breaks.

5. Repeat steps 1 through 4 for the other two bridges.

IN THE REAL WORLD

Drawbridges

A drawbridge is a bridge that can move. Hundreds of years ago, people built wooden drawbridges over moats. The bridges led to castles. People inside could lower or raise the drawbridge. They used ropes or chains. They lowered the bridge so others could enter the castle. They raised the bridge to stop enemies from crossing the moat.

Today, people build drawbridges across large waterways. These bridges are made of steel or concrete. Electric motors raise or lower them. Large ships can pass underneath a raised drawbridge. Cars can cross a lowered drawbridge.

A drawbridge is raised so a boat can pass.

Chapter 3

Results

Thick materials such as craft sticks and cardboard can support more weight than other materials. The aluminum foil is thin. It can sag under the weight of the rocks.

Concrete is a common building material for bridges.

Consider different ways to improve your bridges:

- If the bridge sags, add support under the middle of the bridge. Use cardboard tubes or other materials.
- Try folding the aluminum foil into thicker layers.

Some bridges have sections where cars, trains, and people can pass at the same time.

 Engineers can give bridges unique designs.

- Experiment with the width of the bridge. Can a wide bridge hold more weight than a narrow bridge? Make a guess. Test two bridges of different widths.

Chapter 4

The Science of Bridges

All bridges have a deck, supports, and a **foundation**. **Traffic** crosses a bridge on the deck. Supports hold or lift up the deck. And the foundation supports the whole bridge.

 Cars drive across the deck of a bridge.

Some bridges cross over land. Their foundations go deep into the ground. Other bridges cross over water. Their foundations go in the rock underneath deep water.

Bridges come in different forms. The simplest type is the **girder bridge**. Thick columns or supports stand under either end of a flat beam. They hold it up. **Arch bridges** are similar. Supports hold the deck up. But the supports have a curved shape. In **suspension bridges**, the

 The Samuel Beckett Bridge is a suspension bridge in Dublin, Ireland. It has the shape of a harp.

deck hangs from thick cables. The cables attach to tall towers.

Whatever their shape, all bridges must withstand several **forces**. They must support their own weight and the weight of traffic.

A heavy **load** can cause some parts of the bridge to squeeze together. This force is called compression. At the same time, the load causes other parts of the bridge to stretch. This force is called tension. Builders must balance these forces for the bridge to stand. A strong bridge

Suspension bridges can be damaged by torsion. This force happens when high winds make the deck twist and roll.

FORCES IN BRIDGES

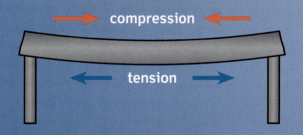

A car weighs down the deck of a girder bridge. The top part of the deck experiences compression. The bottom part experiences tension.

An arch bridge is curved. This shape sends the compression force to the two ends of the curve. There is little tension in an arch bridge.

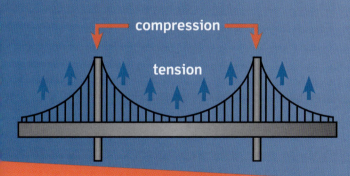

In a suspension bridge, the deck hangs from thick cables held up by tall towers. The cables stretch with tension. The towers are squeezed by compression.

could have helped the gingerbread man cross the river safely.

FOCUS ON
Making a Bridge

Write your answers on a separate piece of paper.

1. How are girder, arch, and suspension bridges the same? How are they different?

2. In what ways do you think bridges are helpful to people?

3. How is the deck of a suspension bridge supported?
   A. The deck is held up by supports.
   B. The deck hangs from wire cables.
   C. The deck is held up by an arch.

4. Why is it important for builders to balance the forces that act on bridges?
   A. If the forces are imbalanced, the bridge might fall down.
   B. If the forces are imbalanced, the bridge will remain standing.
   C. If the forces are imbalanced, the bridge will be effective.

5. What does **sag** mean in this book?

*The aluminum foil is thin. It can **sag** under the weight of the rocks.*

    A. to become flatter
    B. to become lighter
    C. to drop or sink

6. What does **sly** mean in this book?

*A **sly** fox offered to let the gingerbread man ride on his back. Then the fox convinced the gingerbread man to sit on his nose.*

    A. quick
    B. tricky
    C. helpful

Answer key on page 32.

Glossary

arch bridges
Bridges that have the shape of an upside-down U.

forces
Pushes or pulls that happen when one object interacts with another object.

foundation
The supporting base of a structure.

girder bridge
A bridge that has a flat, straight beam held up by supports on either end.

load
A mass or weight supported by something.

span
The full length of something from end to end.

suspension bridges
Bridges in which the deck is supported from above by thick cables.

traffic
The movement of cars or other vehicles along a road or bridge.

withstand
To stand up to a strong force.

To Learn More

BOOKS

Bell, Samantha S. *Building Bridges*. Lake Elmo, MN: Focus Readers, 2018.

Marsico, Katie. *Bridges*. New York: Scholastic, 2016.

Newland, Sonya. *Extraordinary Bridges: The Science of How and Why They Were Built*. North Mankato, MN: Capstone Press, 2019.

NOTE TO EDUCATORS

Visit **www.focusreaders.com** to find lesson plans, activities, links, and other resources related to this title.

Index

A
arch bridges, 24, 27

C
compression, 26–27
concrete, 14, 16

D
deck, 23–27
drawbridges, 16

F
forces, 25–27
foundations, 23–24

G
gingerbread man, 5–7, 9, 27
girder bridge, 24, 27

L
load, 26

S
supports, 23–24
suspension bridges, 24–27

T
tension, 26–27
torsion, 26
traffic, 23, 25

Answer Key: 1. Answers will vary; **2.** Answers will vary; **3.** B; **4.** A; **5.** C; **6.** B